D0551277

I am **NOT** a

Sleepy Sloth

bookoli

Deep in the jungle, high in the trees, the sloths are sleeping, rocked by the breeze.

All except for **one**, who is **wide awake.**

Little Sloth wriggles, and makes her branch **shake.**

Wriggle! Jiggle! Wriggle!

"I'm not sleepy,
I don't need to rest.
Going on
adventures
is what I like best."

Little Sloth lands, and feels rather slow.

She's really not used to being on the go.

But then she **remembers** her arms are **strong,** from hanging on branches for **ever** so **long.**

With a **heave** and a **ho** she **swings** along,
and as she goes, she **sings** this song...

"I may be a sloth
and I may be slow,

but I'm looking for
adventure.
Which way should I go?"

Little Sloth hears a **squawk!** What can it be?

She peeks through the leaves at the top of the tree.

"Wow! Look at me, I've climbed up so high!"

Jungle birds sing as they soar through the sky.

With a **heave** and a **ho,** Sloth swings along, and as she goes she sings this song...

"I may be a sloth and I may be slow, but I'm after **adventure.** Which way should I go?"

HISSSSSS...

Little Sloth's eyes are **wide open** in wonder.

The hiss was made by a **giant anaconda.**

With a **heave** and a **ho**, Sloth swings along,
and as she goes she **sings** this song...

"I never believed I'd meet a snake,

or swing above a swampy lake.

"I may be a sloth and I may be slow, but I'm looking for **adventure**. Which way should I go?"

OOH-OOH-AAH...

A cheeky monkey plays in the river.

Sloth jumps in with a splash and a shiver!

SPLASH!

Now she's swimming, paddling all around,

making a splishy, splashy sort-of sound.

"I never dreamed I would climb so high,

swim so deep or meet the birds in the sky.

But I'm a sloth and I'm feeling dozy.
I need to **rest**,
somewhere
nice and **cozy**."

snoozing and snoring, rocked by the breeze.

"It's great having adventures, flying and leaping! But I love being at home, dreaming and sleeping."